WITHDRAWN

Copyright © 2000 by Nord-Süd Verlag AG, Gossau Zürich, Switzerland
First published in Switzerland under the title *Luftpost für den Weihnachtsmann*
English translation copyright © 2000 by North-South Books Inc.

First published in the United States, Great Britain, Canada,
Australia, and New Zealand in 2000 by North-South Books,
an imprint of Nord-Süd Verlag AG, Gossau Zürich, Switzerland.

Distributed in the United States by North-South Books Inc., New York.

Library of Congress Cataloging-in-Publication Data is available.
A CIP catalogue record for this book is available from The British Library.
ISBN 0-7358-1359-0 (trade binding) 10 9 8 7 6 5 4 3 2 1
ISBN 0-7358-1360-4 (library binding) 10 9 8 7 6 5 4 3 2 1
Printed in Italy

For more information about our books, and the authors and artists
who create them, visit our web site: www.northsouth.com

A LETTER TO
SANTA CLAUS

By Brigitte Weninger
Illustrated by Anne Möller

Translated by Sibylle Kazeroid

A MICHAEL NEUGEBAUER BOOK
NORTH-SOUTH BOOKS / NEW YORK / LONDON

Oliver and his mother lived in a small village high up in the mountains. They were very poor. Oliver's mother was a seamstress, but there was never much work for her. Every day after school Oliver gathered firewood from the hills to sell in the village, but even so, they had only enough money for bare necessities.

One night the baker's wife came to pick up her new dress. She put three coins for Oliver's mother and a little book for Oliver on the table. "It's just an old calendar, but the pictures are really pretty."

"Thank you very much!" said Oliver, beaming.

He sat down with the book next to the flickering lamp and looked at it. He liked the picture for December best. Under the picture was a caption that said: "Every year Santa Claus comes from the North Pole on his sleigh pulled by reindeer and brings gifts for all good children."

For all good children? I never got a present from Santa Claus, thought Oliver. Maybe I wasn't good.

"Mother, what kind of presents are they?" he asked.

"Hmm . . . I think Santa Claus brings children what they wish for," answered Oliver's mother. She rubbed her eyes. "I would wish for a new lamp, so that I would have better light to sew by. Come, Oliver, let's go to bed."

Oliver didn't sleep well that night. He couldn't stop thinking about Santa Claus.

Maybe Santa Claus had never brought Oliver a present because Oliver had never wished for anything. That could be it! But how was Santa Claus supposed to find out what Oliver wanted? It was useless. Sadly, Oliver pulled the blanket over his head.

The next day, Oliver ran into his friend Jacob.

"I brought you a present," whispered Jacob mysteriously, hiding something behind his broad back.

"What is it? Chocolate? Or a little carved horse?" guessed Oliver.

"Wrong! Wrong!" said Jacob, laughing. Just then the moon rose round and red behind Jacob's head.

But no, it was . . . "A balloon!" cried Oliver.

"I bought it for you at the fair," said Jacob. "There's a special kind of air inside that makes it fly."

Carefully, Oliver took the string of the balloon. He was speechless.

Jacob ruffled Oliver's hair and climbed back onto his sleigh.

Oliver continued on his way, entranced.

That afternoon he did not gather any wood. He sat on the fence by the sheep pasture and looked at his balloon.

How beautiful it was! As red as Santa Claus's coat and as round as his stomach. And how it danced in the wind!

If Oliver were to let go of the string, the balloon would fly up into the clouds. Or to the North Pole! Oliver's heart suddenly beat faster.

Maybe the balloon could carry Oliver's wish to Santa Claus! Oliver leaped from the fence and ran home. There he carefully tore a sheet of paper from his school notebook and wrote a letter:

Dear Santa Claus:
My name is Oliver and I am eight years old.
I saw your picture in the calendar and would like
to wish for something. Please bring a new lamp for my
mother. I would like warm boots, because my feet get
so cold in the winter in my wooden shoes. Also
thick mittens, please, because mine are so thin.
If I can have only one wish, please bring
the lamp. I hope you will find me. I live
in Brierley on the mountain.
Please come!
Love from,
Oliver

Oliver folded up the letter and attached it to the string of the balloon. Then he climbed to the top of the mountain above the village.

He looked into the distance for a long time. Where was the North Pole? Should he really let such a wonderful balloon fly away? But it was the only chance he had to find Santa Claus.

Oliver checked the knot on the string one more time. Then he gave the balloon's fat cheek one last kiss and let it go.

But the cold mountain wind wasn't blowing north. Instead it carried Oliver's Christmas balloon to the south, over forests, mountains, and valleys all the way to the sea.
There, on the outskirts of a big city, the balloon was too weak to fly any farther. It bumped over the roof of a house and sank to the garden below.

A little later old Nicholas trudged out of the house and saw the deflated balloon.

"What is this rubbish!" he grumbled. Nicholas was always grumbling ever since his wife had died. It came from being alone so much.

Then Nicholas noticed Oliver's letter. He opened the letter and read it.

"Wishes for Santa Claus!" the old man snorted. "Ha! The things these spoiled brats believe in. Ha! I used to have wishes too."

Nicholas crumpled up the letter and threw it away.

But Nicholas didn't sleep well that night.
He couldn't stop thinking about Santa Claus, and all the things
he had wished for years ago . . . children and grandchildren . . .
and now he was all alone.
And this Oliver, maybe he wasn't such a spoiled brat. Boots,
mittens, and a lamp for his mother—what kind of child wished
for those sorts of things from Santa Claus?
At dawn, Nicholas got up and pulled Oliver's letter out of the
rubbish. Brierley, he thought. Where was that anyway?

Two days later a peculiar man arrived at the station in Urma.
He wore a red coat and had a bag full of packages with him.
Above his head danced a red balloon.
"How do I get to Brierley?" asked the strange man.
"Only by sleigh," answered the stationmaster. "Hey, Jacob,
come here. Will you take this man to Brierley!"

Two hours later there was a knock at Oliver's door.
And then Santa Claus came into the room. Really and truly Santa
Claus! He brought fur-lined boots and nice warm mittens for Oliver.
A bright lamp and a soft shawl for Oliver's mother. Fruit and sweets.
And he also brought back the wonderful Christmas balloon, filled
with air once more!
Santa Claus stayed the whole night at Oliver's. He held Oliver's
hand until he fell asleep, and afterward he talked to Oliver's mother
for a long time. In the morning, they loaded a bundle of clothes,
the new lamp, and the sewing basket into Jacob's carriage and
drove down to the station.

Now Oliver and his mother live with Nicholas.
They call him Grandfather. Every day after school
Oliver plays in the garden, and old Nicholas
laughs happily again.
And every year at Christmas Oliver,
his mother, and Nicholas buy a red balloon.
They write Santa Claus a thank-you note,
tie it to the balloon's string, and let
the balloon fly over valleys, mountains,
and forests all the way to the North Pole.